朋　友

——习近平与贾大山交往纪事

李春雷◎著

中国言实出版社

图书在版编目(CIP)数据

朋友：习近平与贾大山交往纪事 / 李春雷著. -- 2
版. -- 北京：中国言实出版社，2021.2
　　ISBN 978-7-5171-3770-2

　　Ⅰ.①朋… Ⅱ.①李… Ⅲ.①纪实文学—中国—当代
Ⅳ.①I25

中国版本图书馆CIP数据核字（2021）第035722号

出 版 人　王昕朋
责任编辑　肖　彭
责任校对　赵　歌

出版发行　中国言实出版社
　　地　　址：北京市朝阳区北苑路 180 号加利大厦 5 号楼 105 室
　　邮　　编：100101
　　编辑部：北京市海淀区花园路 6 号院 B 座 6 层
　　邮　　编：100088
　　电　　话：64924853（总编室）　64924716（发行部）
　　网　　址：www.zgyscbs.cn
　　E-mail：zgyscbs@263.net

经　　销　新华书店
印　　刷　北京中科印刷有限公司
版　　次　2021 年 3 月第 1 版　　2021 年 3 月第 1 次印刷
规　　格　710 毫米 ×1000 毫米　1/16　6.5 印张
字　　数　106 千字
定　　价　68.00 元　　ISBN 978-7-5171-3770-2

李春雷，河北省成安县人，先后毕业于邯郸学院英语系和河北大学中文系。现为中国报告文学学会副会长、河北省作协副主席。文学创作一级。

主要作品有散文集《那一年，我十八岁》；长篇报告文学《钢铁是这样炼成的》《宝山》等 21 部；

中短篇报告文学《木棉花开》《夜宿棚花村》《朋友——习近平与贾大山交往纪事》等200余篇。曾获鲁迅文学奖、全国五个一工程奖、徐迟报告文学奖等。全国"四个一批"人才，享受国务院特殊津贴专家。

目录

红色岁月 红色历程 红色史诗 红色经典

朋　友
——习近平与贾大山交往纪事

农历癸巳年末，河北作家康志刚在其博客上贴发了中共中央总书记习近平于1998年发表的一篇悼念文章《忆大山》，记述了一段尘封的往事，情真意切，感人肺腑。文章经《光明日报》等多家报刊转载后，引起国人强烈关注。腊月二十三，我赶到正定，拜访了几位当事人。旧事重温，感慨良多……

1982年3月，习近平到正定县任职后，登门拜访的第一个人就是贾大山。

但是，两人的初次见面并不顺利。

关于这次见面的地点和人员，坊间流传多种

说法：有说是在大山家里，有说是在其办公室，有说他正在与众文友聊天，还有文章明言在座者只是李满天。

采访中，笔者曾多方考证，得到的事实是：当天晚饭后，习近平请李满天陪同，一起去寻访大山。先是去家里，不遇，后又赶往其供职的县文化馆。

李满天不是他人，正是经典歌剧《白毛女》故事的第一位记录整理者，时任中国作协河北分会主席，在正定县体验生活，是大山无话不谈的好朋友。

彼时，大山正在办公室里与几个文友讨论作品。他当过老师、编剧、导演和演员，博闻强记，口才极佳。那是一个文学的年代，到处是文学青年，到处是文学论坛。他的屋内，更是常常访客盈门。

李满天是常客了，不必客套，而习近平穿着一件褪色的绿军装，虽然态度谦恭，满脸微笑，但毕竟年轻啊，像一名普通的退伍兵，又像一个青涩的文学青年。或许正是因此，当两人进来的时候，谈兴正浓的大山就没有停止他的演说。

近平悄悄地坐下来，静心地听，耐心地等。

等了一会儿，趁大山喝水的间歇，李满天上前介绍。大山这才明白，面前这位高高大大、清清瘦瘦的青年，就是新来的县委副书记。

接下来，贾大山的反应让习近平印象深刻。2009年7月号出版的期刊《散文百家》，整理发表了习近平2005年回正定考察时的录音："我记得刚见到贾大山同志，大山同志扭头一转就说：'来了个嘴上没毛的管我们！'"尽管这话是大山对着满天压低声音说的。

我们实在无法臆想当时的场景，抑或大山的语气和表情。但可以肯定的是，此时的贾大山还不到40岁，已获得全国大奖，作品收入中学课本，声名正隆，风头日盛，加之天生淡泊清高的性格，面对这个比自己年轻十多岁的陌生的县领导，有一些自负是可以想象的，也是可以理解的。

但是，习近平并没有介意，依然笑容满面。

现场的空气似乎停滞了一下。但不一会儿，气氛就重新活跃起来。主人和客人，已经握手言欢了。

习近平在《忆大山》一文中记录了当时的情景："虽然第一次见面，但我们却像多年不见的朋友，有说不完的话题，表不尽的情谊。临别时……我劝他留步，他像没听见似的。就这样边走边说，竟一直把我送到机关门口。"

那是一个早春的晚上，空气中飘浮着寒意，也一定弥漫着芳香。因为，所有的花蕾，已经含苞待放了……

正定古称常山、真定，春秋时期为鲜虞国。秦立三十六郡，常山有其一。自汉至宋元，真定始终居于冀中南龙首之位，与北京、保定并称

"北方三雄镇"。明清至民初，包括石家庄在内的周围 14 个州县，皆属正定府辖区。

正定城墙周长 24 华里，设四座城门。每座城门均用青条石铺基、大城砖拱券，并设里城、瓮城和月城三道城垣。这种格局十分鲜见，足以说明正定作为京南屏障的特殊地位。高大的城圈内，有九楼四塔八大寺，更有着众多的商铺、戏院、酒肆和茶楼。"花花正定府，锦绣洛阳城"，此之谓也。

古城正定，敦厚、传统且深邃，像一株繁茂的大槐树，绽放着细密的叶芽和花穗，散发着浓郁的清香和氧气。

贾大山 1942 年 7 月生于古城西南街，祖上经营一家食品杂货店铺，家境小富。说起来，他的出世颇具传奇。父母连着生产八个姑娘，直到第九胎，才诞下这个男丁。他从小备受宠爱，吃、穿、玩、乐悉听尊便。他喜欢京剧，爱唱老生，还能翻跟头，拿大顶。他更爱好文学，中学期间便开始发表作品。

高中毕业后，因为出身历史等原因，大山未能走进大学。他先是去石灰窑充当壮工，后又被下放农村。

正是这种特殊的人生际遇，他熟悉了市井文化和农村文化。这两种文化交融发酵，蒸腾升华，促使他成为一名作家。1977 年，他发表短篇小说《取经》，震动文坛，并在首届全国优秀短篇小说评奖中折桂，成为河北省在"文革"之后摘取中国文学最高奖的第一人。无限风光，一时无两。

大山身材中等，体魄壮实。关于他的面貌，他的朋友铁凝曾经有过一段精准的描述："面若重枣，嘴阔眉黑，留着整齐的寸头。一双洞察世事的眼：狭长的，明亮的，似是一种有重量的光在里面流动，这便是人们经常形容的那种'犀利'吧。"

贾大山，的确是一位奇才。

他的创作习惯也迥异常人：打腹稿。构思受

孕后，便开始苦思冥想，一枝一叶，一蘖一苞，苞满生萼，萼中有蕊，日益丰盈。初步成熟后，他便邀集知己好友，集思广益。众人坐定，只见他微闭双目，启动双唇，从开篇第一句话，到末尾最后一字，包括标点符号，全部背诵出来，恰似京剧的念白。他的记忆，犹如一个清晰的电脑屏幕。朋友提出意见后，他仍在腹内修改。几天后，再次咏诵。

三番五次之后，落笔上纸，字字珠玑，一词不易，即可面世。

几天后的一个晚上，贾大山走进了习近平办公室。

关于他们相约的方式和过程，我专门采访当年的县委办公室副主任朱博华和王志敏。他们告诉我，那时没有别的通讯手段，是近平打电话到文化馆，与大山约定的。

县委大院在古城中心，坐北朝南，历史上即

是正定府衙所在。走过门口的两棵老槐树，在过去正堂的位置，是一座主体建筑——穿堂式组合瓦房。瓦房的北面，是两条甬道，甬道中间和两侧，共有三路五排平房，灰砖蓝瓦，南北开窗。近平的办公室兼宿舍，就在西路最前排的东段。

　　只有一间屋子，两条板凳支起一个床铺，一张三屉桌，两把砖红色椅子，一个暖瓶，一盏灯泡。没有书架，成群的书们，或躺在桌面上，或站在窗台上。屋内最醒目的物品，是窗台上的两尊仿制唐三彩：一峰骆驼和一匹骏马，那是北京朋友赠送的纪念品。

　　坐下之后，他们认真地互通了年庚。大山属马，近平属蛇。大山年长 11 岁，自是兄长了。

　　然后，开始一边喝茶抽烟，一边聊天。茶是那种最普通的花茶，烟呢？名曰"荷花"，每包 2 角 6 分钱。聊天的内容由远及近，先是古往今来，国外国内，后来便集中于正定的历史和现实。

　　他们的确有着那么多的相似啊。都曾因家庭

问题而下乡："文革"开始后，年少的近平受父亲
冤案的牵连，挨过批斗，受过关押，到陕北农村
插队时，他还不满16岁；大山也是因为出身商人
之家，被打入另册，1964年即被迁出县城。都在
农村里风雨磨砺：那些年，近平种地、拉煤、打
坝、挑粪，什么累活脏活儿都干过，窑洞里跳蚤
多多，他被咬得浑身水泡；大山一年四季干粗活
儿，秋后种麦拉石砘，两个肩膀红肿如绛。他们
又都在磨砺中收获成果：为了拓广农田面积，寒
冬农闲时节，近平带领乡亲们修筑淤地坝。他还
组织村里铁匠成立铁业社，增加集体收入，后来，
他被群众推举为大队党支部书记；大山在村里担
任宣传员，自编自演了多部小戏，不仅搞活了小
村的文化生活，还多次获得河北省和华北地区文
艺汇演一等奖。

　　最让人称奇的是，他们的知青岁月，竟然都
是七年。

　　对现实问题，他们也有着惊人的相同看法。

比如对正定"高产穷县"的剖析，对如何修复和整理正定文物，对社会上某些不正之风……

两人分手时，已经凌晨三点了。

县委大院已经关闭，门卫的窗户漆黑漆黑。大门两侧是两个高大威武的砖垛，中间是两扇铁门。铁门下部是生硬的厚板，上部是空格的栏杆，足有两米高。

两人面面相觑。夜半天寒，实在不忍打扰熟睡的门卫。

这时，近平蹲下身去，示意大山上去。大山不知所措，却又别无选择，只得手把栏杆，小心翼翼地踩上肩膀。近平缓缓地站起来，像是一台坚实的起重机，托起了大山。大山练过功夫，身手矫健，双手一撑，噌地一下，便翻越而过……

两人相视一笑，隔门道别。

以后的日子里，每隔一段时间就要约见一次。有时是在近平办公室，多数是在大山家里。

晚饭过后，近平安步当车，款款而来。

走出县委大院，沿府前街南行，路东是常山影剧院和百货商店，路西则是一些小商铺、酱菜厂和服装厂。府前街尽头是中山路，西北拐角处便是大山家世代经营店铺的原址。西行20余米，路南是文化馆、印刷厂和建筑公司，北侧则是各种杂货门市和住户。走到育才街，向南300米，左边一个低矮的门楼，便是贾府了。

大山老宅是一个东西狭长的院子，院内有一棵大槐树。夏天到了，槐花如雪，满院馨香。

近平见过大山爱人，颔首，微笑，称一声"嫂子"。

嫂子和大山便把客人迎进北屋。这是大山夫妇的卧室兼会客室，只有十平方米。里面有一床、一柜、一桌、一对沙发和一张茶几。

宾主落座，女主人在茶杯中注满开水后，便到隔壁孩子房间休息去了。

总是有着说不完的话题。

　　大山是地道的正定通，对家乡历史的来龙去脉，每一座塔，每一尊佛都了如指掌。初来乍到的近平，在不长时间内也能对本土文化说古论今、谈笑自若，着实让他刮目相看。大山二十多年来潜心钻研戏曲、文学等，但没有想到的是，近平对这些领域的阅读和思考同样广泛深入，很多见解令人耳目一新。大山年届不惑，历经坎坷，对社会人生深有体悟。然而，比自己年幼十多岁的近平，很多看法竟然不谋而合。大山对近平的尊重之情油然而生，总喜欢同近平交流，也非常看重近平的意见和见解。

　　当然，他们也有着诸多差异。

　　近平看书多且杂，更侧重于政治、哲学和经济，而大山尤专注于文学、史学和佛学；对于现实，近平是一个积极者，即使身处逆境，前途迷茫，他也始终乐观，胸怀梦想。当时，知识青年"返城热"余波未了，城市青年"出国热"高潮渐起，别人都在想方设法地回城或出国，他却主动申请回到农村去，从基层干起。而大山则是一个逍遥派，淡泊名利，无心仕途。他上学时未入团，上班后未入党。省作家协会多次调他去省城工作，他坚决不去，专门为他举办了一次作品研讨会，他居然没有出席。

但大山毕竟是一名作家，职业特点就是关注现实，解剖现实。他得奖的《取经》《花市》等作品，就是以政治视角描写基层干部和普通农民。对这座县城，这个国家，这个民族，他有着深深的热爱和关注，心如烈火燃烧，眼似灯盏明亮。

所以，在根本上，他们又是相同的。

同与不同，相互沟通，互通不同，通而后同。

这样的聊天，不知不觉就到了午夜两三点钟。

为什么总是这么晚呢？他们都是"文革"的过来人，开会到凌晨是家常便饭，而且当时也没有别的娱乐形式，读书，或与好友聊天是知识分子最好的消夜方式了。最关键的，还是他们心意相通，志趣相投，言之有味，言之有物，相守难舍。

出门后，大山会执意相送。于是，他们便接续着刚才的话题，一路边走边聊，直到县委门口。如果大门关闭，大山会自然地蹲下去。这时，近平也不再客气，踩上肩膀，轻手轻脚地翻越过去……

关于他们聊天的日期，我也常常疑问。近平身为县委领导，每天工作繁忙，而且又是嗜睡的年龄。他们相约深谈的时间，是否多在周六晚上？因为只有这样，他才能利用第二天的休息日（当时每周只休星期日一天），补充睡眠。

我曾就此询问时任副县长的何玉女士，她说这属于私人交往，工作日志没有记载。而大山夫人则说，大山没有日记，具体日期无法查询，但他们俩人的熬夜是功夫，经常彻夜不眠，聊到天明。

这期间，正是近平最忙碌的时候。他马不停蹄地奔走于各个公社和大队之间，以最快速度熟悉着县情。

县委有两辆吉普车，他很少乘坐。他总是骑着自行车，穿梭于滹沱河两岸。从河北到河南，是一片大沙滩，常常需要扛着自行车前行。

老干部张五普回忆说："那时我在西兆通公社任书记，他一个人来调研，骑一辆旧自行车，下自行车就和我握手。我问，'习书记怎么你自己来了，你认得路啊？'习书记用衣袖擦一擦满头大汗，说，'打听，我打听着就来了。'"

这一年，习近平办成了一件最令正定人振奋的大事。

正定县是全国闻名的农业高产县，却又是有苦难言的"高产穷县"。多年来，国家规定每年上缴征购粮 7600 万斤，每亩平均负担 200 多斤。由于征购任务过重，很多老百姓口粮不继，不得不到外地购买红薯干度日。习近平了解这些情况后，无比痛心。可要摘掉"高产县"的帽子，无疑是自暴其丑，虽然能够减轻老百姓的负担，县委有关领导却有可能"犯错误"。

是坐等中央调整政策，还是主动向上呼吁？

县委主要领导考虑到习近平刚来工作，不愿让他出面，担心会对他造成不利影响。可习近平说："实事求是向上级反映问题是我党的优良传统，你们不用担心。"于是，他和另一位县委副书记吕玉兰一起，多次跑省进京，向上级部门如实反映正定人民的生活状况和现实困难。

1982年初夏，国务院终于派出调查组。这一年秋后，上级决定把正定粮食征购任务减少2800万斤。

这是一件影响正定历史的大事，为正定农业结构的调整和未来的大发展，奠定了坚实的基础。

在他分抓的领域，更是事必躬亲，脚踏实地。

县委门口的两株古槐，花开花落，几多春

秋，大家熟视无睹。有一次在文化局参加座谈会，近平问槐树是什么年代的。众口无语。他提出请林业专家鉴定。结果竟然是元末明初，是这个古城里年龄最大的植物。于是，围上铁栏，写明文字，加以保护。

城里有一家玉华鞋店，是土地革命时期中共在正定县成立的第一个秘密工人党支部，他指示修缮保护。

"岸下惨案"是 1937 年 10 月日军侵占正定时发生的一起屠杀事件。近平请人挖掘整理，开辟成爱国主义教育基地，并亲自审定纪念碑碑文……

1982 年 12 月 23 日下午，近平打来电话，约大山见面。

"好啊。但是，今天你就不要去机关食堂了，在我家吃晚饭吧。"大山说。交往就要一年了，近平还从来没有在家里吃过一顿饭，作为地主，大山总是自责呢。邀请过几次，他总是笑笑说，君子之交淡如水，我们每次都喝茶水，已经够奢侈了，何必要喝酒呢。今天，大山再次提出了这个请求。

近平怔了一下，居然答应了。

那天晚上，大山准备了几个精致的小菜：雪里蕻炒肉、莲藕片、花生米和凉调菜心。主食呢，就是涮羊肉。没有专用火锅，把铝盆放在蜂窝炉上，权当涮器。虽然器具简陋，但材料却不含糊：麻酱、韭花、蒜末、香菜、酱豆腐一应俱全。

近平如约而至。陪同者仍然是李满天。

炭火红红，蒸气腾腾，几杯小酒下肚，话题也热烈起来，不知不觉就聊到了县文化局。文化局下属剧团、新华书店、文化馆、文保所等七家单位，三四百人，大都是知识分子和演员，情况复杂，矛盾重重。最主要的是，正定有九处国家级文物，这在全国各县中也是屈指可数的，却长久失修，没有发挥应有的作用。

李满天半开玩笑地问："大山，如果让你当局长，能收拾这个摊子吗？"

大山从小与这个圈子打交道，现在又是文化馆的副馆长，自然深知其中矛盾根蒂，于是，借着酒兴，脱口而出："当然可以，只要给我权力，让我说话算数。"接着，便豪情万丈地谈起了自己的"施政纲领"。

这时，近平果断地说："好，就让你当局长！"

大山惊呆了。

原来，针对文化局的乱象，作为县委分管领导，近平一直在暗暗地寻找和选择。正定作为一座历史名城，无论对内还是对外，文化系统都需要一位硬邦邦的领军人物。考虑多日，他和主管文教工作的副县长何玉想法形成一致：最合适的人选只能是贾大山。大山成熟稳健，刚直正派，不仅善写小说，而且也很有行政能力，最关键的是他对文化事业有着近乎痴迷的热爱。但大山不是党员，无意仕途。不过，经过这么多次的深入交往，他对大山的个性又是了解的。于是，在多方征求意见并与主要领导沟通后，在常委会上，他提议大山担任文化局局长，并获得了通过。那天晚上，他就是前来通报的。

近平说："你不能只是自己写小说，还要为正定的文化事业做贡献啊，而且要把你的好作风、好思想带到干部队伍中。"

大山难以置信："可是，我不是党员啊。"那个年代，党外人士在县里担任领导干部，而且是部门正职，是不可想象的。

近平说："你不用担心，组织已经有了安排。"

原来，县委常委会已经形成决议：文化局由局长主持全面工作。

第二天上午，非党人士贾大山，从文化局下属的文化馆副馆长，连升三级，直接上任文化局局长。

正定历史上，这是绝无仅有的！

习近平在《忆大山》一文中，全面评价了贾大山此后几年的工作："上任伊始，他就下基层、访群众、查问题、定制度，几个月下来，便把原来比较混乱的文化系统整治得井井有条。在任期间，大山为正定文化事业的发展和古文物的研究、保护、维修、发掘、抢救，竭尽了自己的全力。常山影剧院、新华书店、电影院等文化设施的兴建和修复，隆兴寺大悲阁、天宁寺凌霄塔、开元寺钟楼、临济寺澄灵塔、广惠寺华塔、县文庙大成殿的修复，无不浸透着他辛劳奔走的汗水。"

士为知己者死。大山是一个文化人，却又是一个血性汉子。

在这里，且讲述几个细节。

常山影剧院，被称为正定的"人民大会堂"，县里重大会议都在此举行。但这座新中国成立之前的木结构建筑，已成危房。近平提议重新建造。为了保证质量，为了保证工期，大山毅然决然地把铺盖搬到工地，日夜监工，虽然他的家就在千米之内。

正定隆兴寺是闻名世界的宋代大型寺院，更是一处国宝级文物。但由于年代久远，破破烂烂。若要全面修复，需要资金3000万元。如此巨大的投资，是当时全国文物系统除了布达拉宫项目之外的第二大工程。为此，近平频频出面邀请国内权威专家前来考察评估，而大山则奔走于京城、省城和县城之间，往返数十趟，直累得心力交瘁，胃肠溃疡。他蜷卧在吉普车后座上，牙关紧咬，冷汗直流。由于长期出差在外，药罐只得带在身边，白天跑工作，晚上熬中药。最后，终于得到上级部门大力支持，落实巨资。

这项浩大的工程，还需要征地60亩，拆迁60户。其中困难，可想而知。

经过千难万难，隆兴寺修复工程终于圆满完成。

至此，隆兴寺真正成为正定最鲜亮的文化名片！

春节期间，是别人最欢乐、最放松的时候，却正是他最紧张、最揪心的时刻。九处国保单位，全是砖木结构建筑，最易着火。每逢此时，他昼夜巡视，废寝忘食。别人劝他，他说："祖宗的遗产，国家的宝物，我负责守护。出一点点问题，我就对不起正定，对不起县委，对不起习书记啊！"……

正定的文化事业进入了新中国成立之后最辉煌的时期。

历史已经证明，贾大山用自己的聪明才智，按照自己的理想，为家乡的文化事业尽到了最大力量。虽然极其苦累，但也极其快活，极其酣畅。

不啻说，贾大山是那个时期全中国最得意、最幸福的文人！

……

这期间，近平升任县委书记，工作更忙了。但他仍然忙中偷闲，一如既往地和大山相约见面，夜聊。

春雨润青，夏日泼墨，秋草摇黄，冬雪飞白。岁月如歌，他们共同享受着友谊的芬芳……

1985 年 5 月的一个午夜，大山已经休息。突然有人敲门，近平请他去一趟。

原来，近平要调走了，第二天早晨 7 时乘吉普车离开。白天交代工作，直忙到半夜，送走所有同事，才腾出时间约见老朋友。好在，这个时间，正是他们最畅快的时光。

关于这一次离别，大山后来从未提起。倒是在近平的笔下，有一段清楚的记载："……那个晚上，我们相约相聚，进行了最后一次长谈。临分手时，俩人都流下了激动的泪水，依依别情，难以言状。"

两人分手时，正好又是凌晨三点。近平最后一次送他到县委门口，四目相对，心底万千话语，口中竟无一言。与往常不同的是，这一次，县委大门敞开着。

采访时，大山妻子告诉我，那天晚上，大山回来时，怀里抱着两尊唐三彩：一峰骆驼和一匹骏马。他一言不发，倒头便睡，直到第二天中午。起床后仍是呆呆地发愣。

妻子以为他病了，催他吃药。他摇摇头，慢慢地说一句："习书记调走了。"

49 岁那一年，大山辞去局长，功成身退，回归文坛。

这个时候，整个文学评论界惊奇地发现，他的小说已经发生了脱胎换骨的蜕变。"梦庄纪事"和"古城人物"系列数十篇短篇小说，微妙而又精确地发掘出文化和人性的敏感共通之处，禅意浓浓，芳香四溢……

大山已经完全醉心于文学。如果说早年的他曾有过文人孤傲的话，那么后期的他，则十足是佛面佛心了，慈眉善目，与世无争，笑看风云，其乐融融。

这其中，有一个细节让人惊叹：大山名闻遐迩，却从无一本著作出版。那些年，文学市场清凉。虽然出版界和企业界不少朋友主动提出帮助，但他笑笑说，不要麻烦你们了，还是顺其自然吧。

贾大山，肯定是当时全中国唯一没有出版过任何图书的著名作家！

他的书房里，悬挂着两句自题诗：小径容我静，大路任人忙。

近平在南方的工作越来越繁重了，但他没有忘记正定，没有忘记大山。每遇故人，都要捎来问候。每年春节，都要寄来贺卡。

但大山却鲜有回应。他知道，他的年轻的朋友，肩上有着太多太多的担负。除了满心的祝愿和祝福，他不忍心有任何打扰。

1995 年底，大山不幸患染绝症，近平十分挂念。1996 年 5 月，他听说大山在北京治疗，便特意委托同事前往探视。春节之前，近平借去北京开会之机，专门去医院看望。近平后来写道："我坐在他的床头，不时说上几句安慰的话，尽管这种语言已显得是那样的苍白和无力……为了他能得以适度的平静和休息，我只好起身与他挥泪告别。临走，我告诉他，抽时间我一定再到正定去看他。"

近平没有食言。仅仅十多天过后，1997 年 2 月 9 日，正是大年初三，他专程赶到正定。在那个他们无数次晤谈的小屋里，两人又见面了。

还是那张桌子，那个茶几，那一对沙发。只是眼前的大山，枯槁羸弱，目光暗淡，再也没有了当年的红光满面和言辞铿锵。

近平强作笑颜，佯装轻松，提议合影。大山说，我这么难看，就不要照相了吧。话虽这样说，他还是努力地坐起来，倚靠在被垛上，挺直身子。近平赶紧凑过去。

11 天后，大山走了。

这是大山在人世间的最后一张留影。陪同他

的，是他的朋友，他的好朋友。

癸巳年末，我去正定采访。

大山的家里，一切依旧，还是三十年前的模样。当年的房屋，当年的木床，当年的书桌，当年的茶几。坐在那里，凝视时空，如幻如梦。恍恍惚惚中，我仿佛看到了当年的影子，隐隐约约里，我似乎听到了那时的笑声。唯有那两尊唐三彩骆驼和骏马，依然新鲜如初，精神而挺拔地伫立着，伫立在时光的流影里，相互顾盼，心照不宣，像一对永恒的朋友……

哦，朋友，朋友，两心如月，冰清玉洁，肝胆相照，辉映你我。

2014 年 2 月 12 日于邯郸学院

Friends

—A Chronicle of the Friendship Between Xi Jinping and Jia Dashan

LI CHUNLEI

Translated by Wang Yanting

At the end of the lunar Gui-Si year[1], Kang
Zhigang, a writer from Hebei Province, posted on
his blog the memorial article Reminisce Dashan
written by Xi Jinping, the current General Secretary
of the CPC[2] Central Committee. Reminisce Dashan
was published in 1998 and recalled a touching past
event genuinely and sincerely. This article attracted
intensive attention from many Chinese after being

---

[1] Around January 2014. All footnotes are added by the
translator.
[2] Communist Party of China.

republished by several newspapers, including Guangming Daily. On December 23 of the lunar calendar[1], I went to Zhengding to interview several people involved in the story of Reminisce Dashan. They were all filled with comprehensive emotions when recalling the past ⋯

The first person visited by Xi Jinping after he took his new official post in March of 1982 in Zhengding County was Jia Dashan. However, their first meeting did not proceed very smoothly.

There are several versions with regards to the place and the attendees of this meeting. Some say it was held in Dashan's home, some say it was held in his office with many literary friends, and others say that it was held in his home with the only additional attendee being Li Mantian.

According to my investigation consisting of

[1] January 23, 2014 of the solar calendar.

various resources and interviews, the truth I have uncovered is that Xi Jinping invited Li Mantian to accompany him that day after dinner to visit Dashan. Failed to find Dashan at home, they then met him at his office in the County Cultural Center.

Li Mantian was the first person who recorded and organized the classic opera The White-haired Girl. He was experiencing the life of Zhengding County as the Hebei branch chairman of the Chinese Writer Association and became one of the best friends of Dashan with no reservations.

At that time, Dashan was discussing their literary works with several literary friends. He had an extraordinary memory and excellent eloquence with a well-rounded life as a teacher, a screenwriter, a film director, and an actor. They were at an era full of literature, full of literary youths, and full of literature forums. Quite often Dashan's office was full of visitors.

As a frequent visitor, Li Mantian bypassed the formal customs, while Xi Jinping wore a faded green army uniform. Although his face carried a courteous smile, his young age made him appear either as an ordinary veteran or as an immature literary youth. This may be the reason that Dashan did not pause his exciting speech when the two came in.

Jinping gently sat down, quietly listened, and patiently waited.

After a while, Li Mantian stepped up to introduce Jinping to Dashan when he took a sip of water. Not until then did Dashan realize that the tall and lean young man was exactly the new vice county secretary of the CPC.

Dashan's following reaction left Xi Jinping with a lasting impression. In July 2009 the journal Hundred Essayists organized and published Xi

Jinping's recollection when he returned to Zhengding for an investigation in 2005: "I remember that the first time I met with Comrade Jia Dashan, he turned his head and whispered to Mantian: a wet-behind-the-ears one was assigned to govern us!"

We can hardly imagine that scene as well as Dashan's tone and emotion. What can be sure is that, at that time, Dashan was still under 40 but had already earned national awards and had his literary works collected in the middle-school textbooks. Adding on his inborn aloofness from politics and material pursuits, along with his raising reputation and popularity, it is imaginable that he had some understandable ambitions in front of unacquainted county leader who was more than ten years younger than him.

Xi Jinping, however, did not mind and still had a full smile on his face.

The atmosphere seemed frozen for a while, but became active again since the host and the guest soon made up.

Xi Jinping recorded this situation in his article Reminisce Dashan: "Although it was the first time we met, we felt like friends separated for many years. We had abundant topics to discuss and endless friendship to express. As I was leaving ⋯ I said it was unnecessary to see me out, yet he paid no attention and was still talking while walking until we reached the gate of the bureau."

It was an early spring night with coldness floating in the air, surrounded by aroma as all the buds were ready to bloom⋯

Zhengding used to be called Changshan, or Zhending, belonging to the Xianyu State during the Spring and Autumn Period[1].During the Qin

Dynasty[2], Changshan was one of the 36 eparchies.

From the Han Dynasty[3] to the Song Dynasty[4] and

the Yuan Dynasty[5], Zhending always occupied the

leading position in central south Hebei and, along

with Beijing and Baoding, was regarded as one of

the three strongest towns in North China. From

the Ming Dynasty[6] and the Qing Dynasty[7] to the

early Republic of China[8], 14 cities and counties

including Shijiazhuang[9] were under the governing

of Zhengding.

The city wall of Zhengding has a perimeter

of 12 kilometers and four gates. Each gate is paved

with green stones and arched with large bricks. It

[1] From 770 B.C. to 476 B.C.
[2] From 221 B.C. to 207 B.C.
[3] From 202 B.C. to 220 A.D.
[4] From 960 A.D. to 1279 A.D.
[5] From 1271 A.D. to 1368 A.D.
[6] From 1368 A.D. to 1644 A.D.
[7] From 1644 A.D. to 1911 A.D.
[8] From 1912 A.D. to 1949 A.D.
[9] Capital city of Hebei Province.

is composed of three sub-walls: Li-Cheng, Weng-Cheng, and Yue-Cheng. This extremely unusual arrangement of the city wall manifests the special status of Zhengding as the south shield for the national capital. Inside the lofty city wall, there are nine buildings, four towers, and eight temples in addition to many shops, theaters, bars, and teahouses, just as described in a poem: "Prosperous Zhengding and Beautiful Luoyang[1]".

The old city of Zhengding is amiable, traditional, and profound, just like a lush Chinese scholar-tree blooming with close tiny buds and spikes, emitting full-bodied scents and oxygen.

Jia Dashan was born in July of 1942 in the Southwest Street of Zhengding to a family who had been operating a grocery store and was moderately rich. His birth was a little legendary as he was the

---

[1] A historically famous city in Henan Province.

ninth child and had eight elder sisters. Therefore, he was spoiled all the time and always satisfied with whatever he wanted to eat, wear, play, and enjoy. He liked Chinese opera and enjoyed playing Laosheng[1], somersault and handstand. What he enjoyed most was literature and he published his works while still in middle school.

After he gradnated from high school, he could not go to college due to his family background; as a result, he became a navvy in a limekiln before being transferred to the rural area.

A special life fortune allowed him to be acquainted with both urban and rural cultures. Those two cultures were mixed, fermented, transpired, and sublimed, inspiring him to be a writer. In 1977, his short story Learning Experiences shocked the literary world and won the championship in the first Chinese

[1] Senior male roles in Chinese opera.

Excellent Short Stories Competition. It was uniquely glorious since he was the first in Hebei Province to win the highest nationwide literature award after the Cultural Revolution.

Dashan had a medium and sturdy stature. His friend Tie Ning had a precise description about his appearance: "His face is scarlet with a large mouth, dark eyebrows, and orderly brush cut. His long narrow and bright eyes can penetrate the world, just like some massy lights are flowing inside, which may match what people often describe as 'incisive'."

Dashan was indeed a prodigy.

His writing habit was also different from ordinary people: he would make a mental draft. With a seed of conception, he started racking his brain with branches, leaves, buds, spikes, calyces, and blossoms of details. After it was roughly down, he would gather friends to collect their comments.

After people sat down, he would gently shut his eyes and open his lips to recite from the first till the last sentences including all punctuations. His memory was like a clear computer screen. He would revise in his mind according to the friends'comments and recite again after several days.

After several rounds of revisions, he would write down the final version without any modifications and with each word a gem.

Dashan visited Jinping's office at night several days later.

To investigate the manner and process of their meeting, I intentionally visited Zhu Bohua and Wang Zhimin, the former vice directors of the county office. They told me that Jinping had made an appointment with Dashan by calling him at the Cultural Center, thc only available communication

红
色
岁
月

红
色
历
程

红
色
史
诗

红
色
经
典

method at that time.

The courtyard of the County Party Committee was located at the center of the old city and faced south, the exact location of the historic Zhengding government. Passing the two old Chinese scholar-trees beside the gate which was located at where the government hall used to be, there was the main building—a hallway style assembly of tile-roofed houses. North of those houses were two corridors, in between and beside which were five arrays of bungalows aligned into three rows with gray bricks, blue tiles and the windows facing north and south. Jinping's office, also his dormitory, was at the east and frontmost part of the west row.

Inside the house, there was only one room containing a bed made of two benches, a desk with three drawers, two brick-red chairs, a thermos bottle, and a light bulb. Since there were no bookshelves, a bundle of books were lying on the desk or standing on the window sill. The most striking decoration was the presence of two mimic Tang sancais[1]: a camel and a horse, souvenirs given by a friend in Beijing.

After sitting down, they seriously told their ages to each other. Dashan was born in the year of the horse[2] and Jinping was born in the year of the snake[3]; as a result, Dashan was the "big brother" as he was 11 years older.

They then started talking while smoking and drinking tea. The tea was the quite ordinary flower tea, and the "Lotus" brand cigarettes cost 0.26 Yuan per package. They talked about the past and the recent, the abroad and the domestic, and finally they were focused on the history and reality of Zhengding.

---

[1] Tri-colored glazed potteries popular in the Tang dynasty (618 A. D. -907 A. D.).
[2] 1942.
[3] 1953.

Their life experiences were so similar. Both had to go to the countryside due to family issues: soon after the Cultural Revolution began, young Jinping, implicated by his father's injustice, was criticized and imprisoned, and was less than 16 when he was forced to settle down in the countryside in Northern Shaanxi Province; Dashan was also discriminated due to his merchant family and was forced to move out of the town. Both were tortured and forged in the countryside: Jinping in those years did all kinds of tiring and dirty works, such as farming, delivering coals, building dams, and carrying mucks, and he was covered in blisters that were the result of being bitten by fleas all over the cave house; Dashan did heavy labors all year long and his two shoulders were severely inflamed from pulling the big stone needed for planting wheat after autumn. Both did, however, benefit from their suffering: Jinping was elected the Party branch secretary of the brigade after he led the fellows building the warp land dam during the winter season to increase the cultivable area, and established the village smiths association to increase the group income; as the village propagandist, Dashan wrote and performed many plays to promote village cultural life and won first places prizes multiple times in the joint cultural performances of Hebei Province, as well as Northern China.

Coincidently, their "educated youth" periods were both seven years.

Their opinions to realistic problems were also unexpectedly identical. For instance, the analysis of why Zhengding was so productive but still poor, the way to repair and organize Zhengding's historic relics, and the attitude towards some bad social tendencies···

It was over 3 am when their conversation had

finished.

The gate was closed and the guard office had no lights shining out of the window. Two iron doors were in between two lofty brick piles beside the gate. The lower parts of the two-meter doors were hard thick planks and the upper parts were hollow railings.

They looked at each other, reluctant to wake up the guard at such a cold winter night.

Jinping then squatted and gestured at Dashan to step on him. Dashan hesitated but had no other choice, so he grasped the railings and carefully stepped on his shoulders. Jinping slowly stood up and hoisted Dashan like a sturdy derrick. Dashan, who had studied Kung Fu, vigorously propped up and flipped over···

They looked at each other and smiled, bidding farewells across the gate.

They met quite often after that day, sometimes in Jinping's office, but more frequently at Dashan's home.

Jinping usually came after dinner by means of a leisurely walk.

Walking out of the County Party Committee courtyard and heading south along the Fuqian Street, the Changshan Theater and the department store were on the east side, and on the west side there were some small shops, the pickles factory, and the garment factory. The Zhongshan Road was at the end of the Fuqian Street, whose northwest corner was where Dashan's family business had been located. About twenty meters heading west, the Cultural Center, the printing house, and the construction company were on the south side, and some grocery stores and residential houses were on the north side.

红
色
岁
月

红
色
历
程

红
色
史
诗

红
色
经
典

Heading south for 300 meters in the Yucai Street, one would find a low rise building on the left side which was Dashan's home.

Dashan's old house consisted of a long narrow courtyard running along the east and west with a big Chinese scholar-tree inside. During summer time, the scholar-tree flowers were snow white and the whole courtyard was permeated with a pleasant flowery fragrance.

Jinping nodded and smiled to Dashan's wife and called her "sister-in-law".

Dashan and his wife guided their guest into the north room, which was both their bedroom and the drawing room. The room was only ten square meters with a bed, a cabinet, a desk, a pair of sofas, and a tea table.

After sitting down, the hostess filled up the tea cups with hot water before resting in the children's room next door.

They always had so much to talk about.

Dashan was a living encyclopedia of Zhengding who knew all the history of his hometown as well as every tower and every Buddha figure in it; as a result, he was amazed by the fact that, after a short time, Jinping, as a new comer, could also leisurely talk about the past and the present of the local culture. Dashan had been diving into opera, literature, etc. for more than twenty years, while he was still surprised by Jinping's equal depth in reading and thinking of those areas. Dashan was over 40 and had experienced many difficulties; as a result, he had a deep understanding of society and human life. Meanwhile, Jinping, who was more than ten years younger, had many opinions that coincided with his. Dashan's respect for Jinping grew immensely; he enjoyed exchanging ideas with him, and also took

Jinping's suggestions and opinions very seriously.

Of course they also had many differences.

Jinping read many books in various fields, especially politics, philosophy, and economics, while Dashan focused on literature, history, and Buddhism. In reality, Jinping was very active, enthusiastic, and ambitious even if facing adversity and a confused future. At that time, the educated youths were still passionate about returning to the urban area from the rural area while the urban youths started raising their interest in going abroad. When others were making their ways to go back to the city or to go abroad, Jinping voluntarily applied to go back to rural area and started his career from the grass roots. In contrast, Dashan believed in peripateticism and paid no attention to fame, wealth, or an official career. He neither joined the Youth League in school nor joined the CPC as a worker. He refused several times the assignment of relocating to work in the provincial capital offered by the Provincial Writers Association, and even did not appear at the workshops discussing his literary works.

Nevertheless, as a writer, Dashan's professional characteristics were those of paying close attention to reality and analyzing this reality. His works, such as Learning Experiences and Flower Market, depicted grass-root cadres and ordinary peasants. He deeply loved and closely followed this town, this country, and its people with his heart burning like a blaze and his eyes as bright as lamps.

Therefore, they were identical at the most basic founding level.

They were identical yet different; as a result they communicated with each other to figure out their differences and then would proceed to agree with each other after their discussions.

These kinds of discussions unwittingly lasted until 2 or 3 am.

Why always so late? Well because they both experienced the "Cultural Revolution", a time when people had been used to hold meetings until dawn. In addition, there were no other ways to entertain themselves. Reading or chatting with friends was the best way for intellectual people to spend the night. The best way for sharing and spreading knowledge was to spend the night by either reading or chatting with friends. More importantly, they understood each other, had common interests, enjoyed each other's speeches, and thus enjoyed staying together.

Dashan insisted insist on walking Jinping out after their discussions. They then continued to discuss the previous topics while walking until they reached the gate of the County Party Committee. Dashan would naturally squat if the gate was closed and Jinping would step up onto his shoulders without hesitation and quietly flip over the gate···

I often questioned the validity of the dates on which their discussions were held. Jinping was very busy as a county leader and was at the age in need of an abundant amount of sleep. As it was the only way in which he could gain more sleep the next morning, could they have possibly met and chatted most often on Saturday nights? (Sunday was the only off day during the week at that time.)

I asked this question to Ms. He Yu, who had been a deputy county magistrate at that time. She explained that, as private communications, their meetings had not been recorded in the working dialogs. On the other hand, Dashan's wife said that the dates could not be tracked since Dashan did not write diaries; however the two were both good at standing late at night and quite often chatted without sleep until dawn.

This period of time was the busiest days for Jinping. Jinping ceaselessly traveled among different communes and brigades in order to familiarize himself with the situation of the county as quickly as possible.

He seldom took the two jeeps provided by the County Party Committee. Instead, he always shuttled between the two banks of the Hutuo River by bicycle. He had to lift the bicycle when going over the big sand beach between the north and south sides of the river.

Zhang Wupu, one of the old cadres, recalled: "At that time I was the Party secretary of Xizhaotong Commune. Jinping came alone to investigate by riding an old bicycle and shook my hands immediately after he got off the bicycle. I asked:

'Secretary Xi, why did you come by yourself? Did you know the route?' Secretary Xi wiped off the sweat all over his head with his sleeves and said: 'Asking. I came by asking people the route.' "

In that year, Xi Jinping managed to accomplish a task which was most impressive to the Zhengding people.

Zhengding was a famous county nationwide due to its high agricultural yield, yet ironically it was also a "high-yield poor-county" with its suffering hard to tell. For many years the central government ordered the county to submit 76 million jin[1] of grain to be purchased by the state, which was on average more than 200 jin per mu[2]. Because the state-purchase duty was so heavy, many people did not have enough food and had to buy dried sweet potatoes from other places. Xi Jinping was greatly

---

[1] One jin is equal to half a kilogram.
[2] One mu is equal to 0.165 acres.

mortified after becoming aware of this situation. However, it would be self-degrading to dispel the honor of a "high yield county" and the responsible county leaders would possibly be regarded as having "made a mistake", even though doing so would lift the burden placed on the county people.

Was it best to just passively wait for a policy change to be put forward by the central government, or was it best to voluntarily appeal for a policy change?

The chief leader of the County Party Committee did not want Xi Jinping to take charge of this problem as he had just been instated and doing so might impact him negatively. However, Jinping said: "You do not have to worry since it is our party's fine tradition to report problems honestly to the higher authorities." Along with Lv Yulan, another vice secretary of the County Party Committee, he went many times to the provincial capital, as well as Beijing, to report to the higher authorities the living conditions and real difficulties of the Zhengding people.

In the early summer of 1982, the State Council finally sent out an investigation group to Zhengding. After that autumn, the higher authorities decided to deduct 28 million jin from the state-purchase grain requirement.

This event had historic importance since it formed the basis for adjusting Zhengding's agricultural structure and prosperous development in the future.

With regards to the fields that Jinping was in charge of, he was involved in everything personally and was earnest and down-to-earth.

There were two old Chinese scholar-trees in front of the County Party Committee courtyard for many years and people were used to their cycle of blossoming and withering. Once in a symposium held in the Bureau of Culture, Jinping asked in which era those two trees had sprouted. Nobody was able to answer, so he proposed to invite botanists to identify their time of sprouting. The two trees turned out to have sprouted in the late Yuan or early Ming dynasty, making them the oldest plants in the county. They were thus protected, surrounded by iron fences and tagged with signs.

Jinping also ordered the repair and protection of Yuhua Shoe Shop in town, where the first secret workers'Party branch in Zhengding had been founded during the Agrarian Revolution period.

"Anxia Massacre" was a tragic event which occurred in October of 1937 when the Japanese army invaded Zhengding. Jinping had the materials related to the incident excavated and sorted out for

the purpose of building a patriotism education base.
Jinping personally examined the monumental text⋯

In the afternoon of December 23, 1982, Jinping
called Dashan to arrange a meeting.

"OK, but don't go to the dining hall, just come
to my home to have the dinner." Dashan said. As a
host, Dashan always blamed himself that Jinping
hadn't had a dinner at his home. Actually he invited
Jinping several times, but Jinping always replied
with smile: "the friendship between gentlemen is as
pure as water. It is already luxurious that we drink
tea each time, so it is unnecessary to drink wine."
That day, Dashan again expressed his invitation.

Jinping unexpectedly accepted the invitation
after hesitating for a while.

That night Dashan prepared several exquisite
small dishes: pork with potherb mustard, lotus root
slices, peanuts, and cold cabbage heart dressed with

sauce. The main dish was mutton in hot pot. There was no specialized hot pot, instead an aluminum basin was put above the honeycomb briquette stove. Although the container was crude, the ingredients were excellent: sesame paste, Chinese chive paste, minced garlic, coriander, and fermented bean curd, well stocked with food of all kinds.

Jinping arrived on time, and as always Li Mantian was accompanying him.

With flaming charcoal fire and rising steam, the topic of their passionate discussion unwittingly migrated to the County Bureau of Culture after several rounds of drinking. The Bureau of Culture administered seven entities including the theatrical troupe, the Xinhua Bookstore, the Cultural Center, and the Relic Protection Institute. Most of the three to four hundred employees were intellectuals and actors with complex relations and contradictions.

Most importantly, Zhengding had nine national-level relics, which was rare in all counties nationwide, yet they were in very poor condition due to a long-time lack of proper maintenance.

Li Mantian asked half-jokingly: "Dashan, would you be able to tidy it up if you were the bureau chief ?"

Dashan had been inside that community since he was a kid and he was the vice manager of the Cultural Center at that time, so he had a good understanding of the contradictions inside that community. He replied instantly by taking advantage of the revelry: "I would if I were given the power to make such decisions." Then he described with lofty sentiments his "policy outlines".

Jinping then decidedly said: "All right. The bureau chief you are!"

Dashan was astonished.

Actually, facing the messy situation of the

County Bureau of Culture, as the leader in charge, Jinping had been secretly looking for a new bureau chief. As a historically famous city, Zhengding needed an excellent leader in the cultural system to undertake both inside and outside affairs properly. After considering for many days, he reached an agreement with He Yu, the deputy county magistrate who was in charge of culture and education, that the best candidate was Dashan. Dashan was mature, steady, rigid, and decent. He was not only specialized in writing stories, but also had good administrative abilities, and most importantly, he was almost obsessively in love with cultural undertakings. However, Dashan was neither a Party member nor aspired to have an official career. Nevertheless, Jinping was familiar with Dashan's personality after their in-depth interactions for so many times. Therefore, after soliciting the opinions of various people and communicating with the major county leaders, his proposal of promoting Dashan to be the chief of the County Bureau of Culture was approved in the standing committee conference. He was announcing this news to Dashan at that night.

Jinping said: "You should not only write stories by yourself, but also contribute to the cultural undertakings of Zhengding. You should also bring your good working style and mentality into the cadre team."

Dashan replied unbelievably: "But, I am not a Party member." At that time, it was unimaginable to have a non-Party-member serving as a county leader, especially as a department head.

Jinping said: "You do not have to worry. The organization already has everything arranged."

In fact, the county standing committee already passed the resolution that the bureau chief would be in total charge of the Bureau of Culture.

The next day, Jia Dashan, a non-Party-member, was directly advanced three ranks from the vice manager of the Cultural Center, a subunit of the Bureau of Culture, to the chief of the bureau.

This was a one-of-a-kind event in the history of Zhengding!

Jinping, in his article Reminisce Dashan, made an overall assessment of Dashan's work in several years afterwards: "When his duties had just begun, he went to the grass-root units, visited the masses, investigated problems, and established regulations. The messy cultural system was renovated and reinstated to be in good order. As the incumbent, he tried his best to develop Zhengding's cultural undertakings and to study, preserve, maintain, unearth, and save cultural relics. He put great effort into constructing and restoring cultural facilities such as the Changshan Theater, the Xinhua Bookstore, and the cinema, as well as the Dabei Loft of the Longxing Temple, the Lingxiao Tower of the Tianning Temple, the bell tower of the Kaiyuan Temple, the Chengling Tower of the Linji Temple, the Hua Tower of the Guanghui Temple, and the Dacheng Palace of the county Confucian temple."

A true gentleman will sacrifice himself for a friend who understands him. Dashan was not only a scholar but also loyal to his friends.

Just several details are described here.

The Changshan Theater was regarded as "the Great Hall of the People" of Zhengding with all important county conferences held there. However, it became a dilapidated building since the wood-frame was built even before the foundation of new China. Jinping proposed to construct a new one. To ensure the construction quality and to meet the deadline, Dashan determinedly lived at the construction site to supervise day and night although his home was within one kilometer.

The Longxing Temple of Zhengding, a national treasure, was a world-famous large temple built during the Song Dynasty. Fully restoring this ancient and shabby temple would cost 30 million Yuan, the second largest project, just after the Potala Palace[1], in the national cultural system. For this project, Jinping frequently invited domestic experts to inspect and evaluate, while Dashan traveled between Beijing, the provincial capital, and the county tens of times and was mentally and physically exhausted with stomach and intestine ulcers. Dashan lay down in the backseat of the Jeep with clenched teeth and cold sweat. As Dashan was out of town most of

[1] The largest temple located in Tibet.

the time, he had to bring the Chinese medicine pot with him and boil the medicine at night after work. Finally, the higher authorities supported Dashan and Jinping by granting them a huge fund.

This vast project had imaginable difficulties, including taking over 60-mu land for use and relocating 60 houses.

After overcoming thousands of difficulties, finally the project of the Longxing Temple restoration was successfully accomplished.

Not until then was the Longxing Temple considered the most brilliant cultural symbol of Zhengding!

The Chinese New Year was supposed to be the happiest and most relaxing time, but to Dashan, it was the most nerve-racking and anxious period. All nine national preservation relics were very susceptible to burning down since they were built from brick and wood. At times like this, he patrolled day and night without rest. When somebody tried to persuade him to take a rest, he replied: "I have taken the responsibility of guarding those heritages left by ancestors which are also national treasures. In case a little accident happened, how could I face Zhengding, the county committee, and Secretary Xi!"

The cultural undertakings of Zhengding entered the most glorious period since the foundation of new China.

History has manifested that Jia Dashan tried his best to develop the cultural undertakings of his hometown with his intelligence and wisdom, guided by his ideals. Although extremely exhausting and tiring, it was also extremely joyful.

There is no doubt that Dashan was the most beamish and blessed scholar in the whole country!

...

During this time, Jinping became busier as he was promoted to be the county Party secretary; however, he still managed to find some time to meet with Dashan to chat at night.

Spring rain moistened green plants; summer sunshine graced the earth; yellow autumn grass swung; and white winter snow flied. The years went by like songs and they both enjoyed the fragrance of friendship ···

At the midnight of May 1985, after Dashan was already in bed, somebody suddenly knocked at his door and told him that Jinping had invited him to meet.

It turned out that Jinping would leave by Jeep in the next morning at 7 am due to a promotion. He was busy with the handing over process all day long up until midnight, and it was only then that he had time to meet with his old friend after saying goodbye to all of his colleagues. Fortunately, that was the time they enjoyed being together the most.

Dashan never mentioned that moment of farewell, but Jinping wrote down some details: "⋯ At that night, we gathered together and had our last long conversation. When the time to say goodbye came, we were both moved to tears and the feeling of unwilling to be apart was beyond words."

It was again 3am in the morning when they bade farewell. Jinping sent him to the gate of the County Party Committee for the last time. Standing face to face, they were speechless although they had enormous inmost words. The difference was that this time the gate was open.

During the interview, Dashan's wife told me that when Dashan came back at that night, he held in his arms two Tang sancais: a camel and a horse. He went to sleep without saying a single word and was still in a daze when he woke up at the next noon. She pushed him to take medication as she thought he was sick. He shook his head and said slowly: "Secretary Xi left Zhengding."

When he was 49 years old, Dashan resigned from his position of bureau chief and came back to the literary world after a successful official career.

The literary critics surprisingly found that his stories had a complete reborn transition at that time. Many of the short stories in the two collections, The Chronicle of Mengzhuang and The People in the Old City, delicately and accurately dag out the sensitive commonness between culture and humanity with luscious Buddhism and abundant fragrance…

Dashan was completely devoted to literature. If

he had used to, as a scholar, be aloof and proud, then in the rest of his life he was purely a Buddhist with a benignant look, philosophical resignation, a steady mind, and peaceful happiness.

An amazing fact was that Dashan had no single book published despite his far-spreading fame. The literature market was stagnant in those years. Although many friends in the publishing and enterprise industries offered him help with publishing, he always smiled and replied: "Don't bother. Let it be."

Dashan was for sure the only famous writer in the whole country without any books published!

A two-sentence self-written poem was on the wall of his study room: "Small alleys allow me to be serene. Big roads are for busy people running."

Jinping was even busier with heavy duty in the south, but he did not forget Zhengding and Dashan.

He sent his regards whenever he met with a local friend and mailed greeting cards in every Chinese New Year.

However, Dashan seldom replied because he knew that his young friend was so busy with many responsibilities. He did not have the heart to bother him in anyway except sincerely wishing and blessing for him.

By the end of 1995, Dashan was unfortunately terminally ill and Jinping was seriously concerned. In May 1996, after he heard that Dashan was under treatment in Beijing, he intentionally arranged a colleague to visit Dashan on behalf of him. Before the Chinese New Year, Jinping purposely visited Dashan in the hospital when he went to Beijing for a business trip. Jinping later on wrote: "I sat on the edge of his bed and comforted him from time to time, although those words appeared so pale and weak… I had to stand up and leave with tears so that he could have some undisturbed rest. Before I left, I told him that I would find some time and visit him in Zhengding."

Jinping did not break his promise. On February 9, 1997, the third day of the Chinese New Year, he purposely visited Zhengding. They met again in the small room where they had chatted for countless times.

The desk, the tea table, and the pair of sofas were still the same. The only difference was that Dashan in front of him was withered and weak with bleak eyes, and the previous glowing appearance and sonorous voice had long gone.

Jinping pretended to smile and be relaxed; and proposed to take a photo together. Dashan refused by saying that he was bad looking, but at the same time tried hard to sit up straight by leaning on the quilt.

Jinping hurried to move closer.

Dashan passed away eleven days later.

That was the last photo of Dashan when he was alive, accompanied by his friend, his best friend.

I went to Zhengding for an interview at the end of 2013.

Dashan's home was exactly the same as it had been 30 years ago. That house, that wooden bed, that desk, and that tea table; sitting there and staring at the space and time, I felt unreal and dreamy. Dazedly I seemingly saw their shadows and indistinctly I likely heard their laughs. Only the two Tang sancais, the camel and the horse, were still as fresh and stood vigorously. They stood inside the shadow of flowing time, looked at each other, and tacitly understood each other, just like a pair of eternal friends ⋯

Oh, friends, friends, with two moon-like hearts,

红
色
岁
月

红
色
历
程

红
色
史
诗

红
色
经
典

pure and noble, devoted to each other, and shining

for each other.

Written at Handan College

February 12, 2014

创作感言

别有用心

——《朋友》创作感言

———

李春雷

2013 年底，河北作家康志刚在博客上贴发习近平总书记《忆大山》一文之后，经《光明日报》转发，在全国引起强烈反响。河北省作协党组特别重视，希望我深入采访，写一篇报告文学。

采访时已经腊月二十三。我在正定住了三个夜晚，约谈了十多位老同志。采访结束时，我还沿着当年习近平总书记拜访贾大山的行走路线，认认真真地走了一遍，寻找感觉。

回到家后，我就下决心闭门谢客，放弃过年！于是，我关掉手机，只在半夜时看一看信息。这个年，我没有见一个朋友，没有喝一杯酒。每天在书房里，直写得头晕脑涨，连上下楼也感觉是在云里雾里。

实际上，最难的还不是身体上的苦累，而是思考上的迷茫，和试图突破又难以突破的痛苦。因为这是一个全新课题，主人公不是一般人物。所以，我必须调整自己的视角，调动自己的一切储备。

过去，对于领袖人物，我们总是自觉不自觉地习惯于高大全，而恰恰这种写法，让作品脱离了群众，远离了人气。所以，我把总书记当作一个普通人来写，写出生活中、工作中本色的他。他与大山是朋友，与我们也是朋友。所以，在文中，除了必要的时候，我大都是直呼其名。

说到报告文学的真实性，其实也是相对的。《史记》中的精彩章节，司马迁明显带有个人感情色彩并有虚构。再比如《哥德巴赫猜想》，其中一些细节也不乏争议。但在《朋友》里，不能有任何虚构和想象。即使是一些有确切文字记载的史实，我也要慎重地选择使用。

孔子说，言之无文，行之不远。我在坚守真实性的同时，特别注意艺术性。在整体行文叙述中，多借鉴古典小说、古典散文的笔法，变换视角，开开合合，杂以闲笔，多用短句；在结构布局上，我追求一种自然、浑圆的感觉，看似随意，实则用心。

说到用心，在文章的思想性方面，我更是别有用心。

作为一个现实主义作家，面对当前这个不尽如人意的社会生态，我试图提供一些思考：比如，从尊重文化、尊重人才的角度，从勤于读书、善于学习的角度，从勤政廉政、干事创业的角度；再比如，从端正友谊、完善人格的角度。我认为，总书记都为这个时代树立了一个光辉典范，具有特殊的现实意义。

同时，写作之初，我也有一个梦想，那就是创造一个成语，像高山流水、管鲍之交、三顾茅庐等历史上的著名成语故事一样，为中华文明史留下一段佳话。我曾设想这个成语叫"正定之交"或"午夜之交"，但不合适。网上有人已经命名"习贾之交"，也太直白。总之，这是一段千载难逢的友谊故事，是古代经典故事在现实生活中的翻版和提升。我相信，肯定会有一个最恰当最准确的成语，把这个故事表达出来，流传下去。

专业评论

习贾之交　辉映你我

——著名作家李春雷谈《朋友》创作前后

———

　　4月21日，著名作家李春雷的纪实文学《朋友——习近平与贾大山交往纪事》被新华社以通稿形式发表，《光明日报》《人民日报》《中国青年报》《经济日报》等近千家报刊相继转载，在海内外引起强烈反响。

　　据悉，新华社以通稿形式发表一篇文学作品，《光明日报》在头版头条刊登一篇文学作品，在其历史上均属首次。而且，一部文学作品在短时间内被近千家报刊转载，这种现象也是前所未有。《光明日报》连续发表四篇评论文章，认为《朋友——习近平与贾大山交往纪事》"突出了厚德载物的责任感和使命感，彰显了以核心价值观为内涵的中国精神，树立了领导干部交友的光辉典范，展现了纪实文学独特的艺术魅力"。香港《华夏纪实》总编辑王彤认为"《朋友——习近平与贾大山交往纪事》具有深刻独特的思想意义和精妙绝伦的艺术价值，是一篇不折不扣的传世名篇"。

　　近日，本报联系作者，请他讲述作品背后的故事。

（一）千载难逢的友谊

2013 年 10 月，河北文学馆改陈布展，偶然发现习近平同志于 1998 年在《当代人》杂志上发表的一篇悼文《忆大山》，情真意切，十分感人。省作协党组书记魏平是一位"老宣传"，马上意识到这篇文章的珍贵及其独特的现实意义，便请文章的责任编辑康志刚贴发在其博客上。

果然，该文引起《光明日报》关注，于 2014 年 1 月 13 日转载，立时引起社会广泛关注。

但是，受限于篇幅和角度，该文并没有展开。我和很多读者一样，感觉意犹未尽。这时候，魏平同志找到我，希望深入采访，创作一篇纪实文学。于是，春节之前，我赶赴正定。

由于有组织介绍，正定方面勉强接待了我。原来，总书记去年 7 月来访时，出于谦虚和低调，曾半开玩笑地说过，他在正定工作时的事情不要过多宣扬。这毕竟是总书记的嘱托。不过，他和贾大山的真情故事，在正定早已不是秘密，只是流传着几个版本。

鉴于故事真实存在，又实在是正能量，而且也实在有必要正本清源。我采访时，几位当年的知情人一起坐下来，认真地、反复地回忆，多方佐证、考实，基本还原了当年的真貌。

在正定的最后一天夜里，我特地沿着总书记当年拜访贾大山的行走路线，又细细地踩踏了一遍，寻找感觉。

通过采访，我进一步受到触动。从习近平上任后的第一次登门拜访，到贾大山人生最后时刻的最后一次登门探望，这个故事真实、感人且完整，是任何天才作家也虚构不出来的。而且，它拥有着独特的现实意义，和永久珍贵的历史价值。

于是，我决心打破传统，用纯正的文学笔法去书写，为历史留下最真实、最精美的记忆。

但是，当真正动手创作时，却发现困难如山。这是一个全新课题，主人公又是特殊人物。自从改革开放以来，国内作家用文学笔法描写在任最高领导人，还从未有过。

（二）严苛的真实性

过去，对于领袖人物，我们总是自觉不自觉地习惯于高大全，写他们的伟岸与光辉，而恰恰是这种写法，让很多作品脱离了群众，淡薄了人气。所以，创作之初，我就下定决心，从人情人性的角度切入，写出生活中、工作中本色的习近平。他与大山是朋友，与我们也是朋友。他的微笑和真诚是面对大山的，也是面对大家的。所以，在文中，除了必要的时候，我大都直呼其名：近平。

说到纪实文学的真实性，其实也是相对的。比如《史记》中，描写陈胜、项羽和刘邦等人的场景和对话，写到将相和、鸿门宴和霸王别姬，司马迁明显带有个人感情色彩并有虚构。再比如《哥德巴赫猜想》，写到党支部书记给陈景润送苹果，是在成功前还是成功后，存有争议。

但在《朋友——习近平与贾大山交往纪事》里，不能有任何虚构和想象。比如习贾第一次相见的地点和在场人员，现有报道中众说纷纭，有说在贾家，有说在文化馆；有说习独自寻访，有说在座者许多人，有说在座者只有李满天。采访时，我反复考证，最后确认：习请李陪同，先去贾家，不遇，又去文化馆。

又如习近平唯一的那次去贾家用餐的具体时间，过去都语焉不详。我感觉这是一个重要节点，应该尽量交代清楚。于是，我多方查找资料，最后在该县原文保所所长的日记中，确认是 1982 年 12 月 23 日下午。

还有更多材料，我全部依据当事人的口述或文字，并进行交叉印证。

（三）两进中南海

节后上班，我将作品送交省作协党组。

党组提出意见并修改后，报送《光明日报》社。报社十分重视，审阅通过后，按有关程序于 2 月 12 日报送中央办公厅。

但在后来的两个多月里，没有音信。我以为作品就此永远休眠了。毕竟题材太特殊了。而且，中办通行公文体，而我是文学语言，他们能认同吗？还有，文内的称呼大都是"近平"，是否会有犯忌？

正当我心灰意冷之时，北京方面通知我进京面谈。

于是，我心怀忐忑，第一次走进了中南海。

会面在中南海内部一个小型会议室进行。出乎我意料的是，中办有关人员首先肯定了作品。而后，他们提出几点修改意见，大致有三：文中应对李满天这个人物更多着墨；建议在写法上略加修改，一些闲笔要适当删节；文内一些语句要认真推敲斟酌。

李满天原名林漫，是经典歌剧《白毛女》故事的第一个作者，时任中国作家协会河北分会主席，在正定县挂职县委常委，是习贾相识的见证人。

本文是文学作品，不是新闻宣传，所以我借鉴了古典散文的笔法，看似闲笔，实则别有用心，是在不动声色地交代叙事，更是在增加艺术效果。如果直白直露，文学品质就会减损。

在其后的一周时间内，就以上问题，我和负责审核稿件的同志通了无数次电话，又相约第二次面商。

可以说，文内每一个句话，都进行了反复推敲。不能模糊，不含虚浮，都要言之有据，准确适当。比如原文写到习贾初见时，我这样表述："习近平到正定县任职后，拜访的第一个人就是贾大山。"此句虽然突出了习近平尊重人才、思贤若渴的心情，但细细想来，并不精确。设想，一位县委副书记上任后，首先拜访的应该是主要领导、同事或老干部，怎么能是一位基层文化工作者呢。在对方的建议下，我在"拜访"之前加上两个字："登门"。这样一来，就合情合理了。

又比如，在写到近平到南方工作后，每年都寄来贺卡，而贾大山为了不打扰朋友，鲜有回应。在此，我原文写到"他知道，他的年轻的朋友，是属于这个国家的，是属于这个民族的"。但那位同志说，当时习只是福建省委副书记，这样用语显然不妥，即使当时大家都看好他的前程，即使他现在果然担任了党的最高领导人。于是，改为"他的年轻的朋友，肩上有着太多太多的担负"。

审核部门的认真和严谨，让我惊叹。这一点，的确值得学习！

我最担心的是写作方法上的改弦易辙。如果那样的话，这篇作品的文学价值就丧失了。庆幸的是，在我的再三解释下，他们最终尊重了我的意见。

最费周折的还是李满天。在我精心设计、增加笔墨后，中办又提出一个问题：核对李满天与林漫的关系。李满天原名李春芳，创作《白毛女》时，曾用名林漫，在正定任职时，也沿用此名。而从1980年当选中国作家协会河北分会主席始，正式用名李满天，直至去世。虽然明知两个名字系一个人，但中办明确指示，要找到权威记载。李满天已于1990年作古，档案杳无影踪。我马上请正定方面从组织档案中查找。但他们查遍档案，却无李满天其人其名。我找来一本正定县志，终于找到了林漫的任职记载。但怎样证明两名系一人呢？我请教省作协魏平书记。她告诉我，李满天的儿媳妇就在省作协财务处工作，可请她出证明，再由省作协盖章。

（四）破格发表

说到发表，实在出乎预料。此稿由《光明日报》报送中办，原计划在该报首发。

4月20日中午，我忽然接到中宣部新闻局电话，告知稿子正在履行程序，可能近日发表。

当天傍晚18时30分左右，我收到南京一位朋友短信，说在新华网上看到《朋友——习近平与贾大山交往纪事》。我马上查看，果然占领了各大网站头条。夜半时分，正在办公室值班的《光明日报》总编辑何东平请我回复电话。他告诉我，以新华社通稿形式发表效果更好，并向我表示祝贺。

刚放下电话，又发现省作协魏平书记欣喜地发来短信。我马上打过去，向她表示感谢。

第二天，全国很多报纸纷纷刊发《朋友——习近平与贾大山交往纪事》。后来，据不完全统计，有数百家之多。

20世纪60年代初，《县委书记的榜样——焦裕禄》由新华社通稿播发，红遍全国。但据考证，该稿播发时体裁为长篇通讯，署名为新华社记者穆青等三人。

如此，《朋友——习近平与贾大山交往纪事》应是新华社历史上以通稿形式播发的第一篇文学作品。

（五）正定之交

说到《朋友——习近平与贾大山交往纪事》的思想性，我确实别有用心。

作为一个现实主义作家，在当前这个不尽如人意的社会生态中，我试图通过总书记与贾大山的"正定之交"给社会特别是官场提供一些思考。无论从尊重文化、尊重人才的角度，从勤于读书、善于学习的角度，还是从勤政廉政、干事创业的角度，抑或从端正友谊、完善人格的角度。当然，如果从党的群众路线教育实践活动的角度，则更具现实意义。

同时，写作之初，我还有一个梦想：那就是创造一个成语，像高山流水、管鲍之交、三顾茅庐等历史上的著名成语一样，为中华文明史留下一段佳话。我曾设想这个成语叫"午夜之交"，但不合适。文章发表后，网络上有人注册"习贾之交"，也有些直白。现在我倒是觉得"正定之交"更有表现力，又具地域色彩，也通俗易记。总之，这是一段千载难逢、感人至深的友谊故事，是古代经典故事在现实生活中的翻版和提升。我相信，肯定会有一个最恰当最准确的成语，把这个故事表达出来，流传下去。

当然，我还有一个梦想，就是用文学的力量进一步光大习近平总书记的形象：不仅雄才大略，见筋见骨，而且儒雅慈祥，有情有义，有血有肉，极富人情味儿。

习近平总书记上任后，展示给世界的更多是前一种形象，而这一篇文章展示的则是后一种。两者结合起来，才是真正的中国领袖形象！我相信，这种形象应该是立体的，有正面的，有侧面的；有政治的，有经济的，有军事的，更有文化的。而文化，是最深入人心的。

近日，美国《时代周刊》高度评价了习近平的执政风格和理念，并预测他将成为"中国第一位真正的全球领袖"。这些天，我也注意到，西方媒体对《朋友——习近平与贾大山交往纪事》格外关注，也比较认同。这其中就包含着这种文化因素吧。

（原载于《中国纪检监察报》2014 年 10 月 13 日）

高山流水奏新声

——读李春雷的《朋友——习近平与贾大山交往纪事》

——

彭　程

　　读李春雷的纪实文学《朋友——习近平与贾大山交往纪事》，先之以感动，继之以感慨，思绪萦绕，浮想联翩。掩卷良久，心情依然难以平复。作品描写的是 20 世纪 80 年代初，习近平同志任河北正定县委书记期间与作家贾大山的交往，和两人结下的深厚友谊。阅读的过程中，不由自主地想到了那一个个流传至今的关于友谊的美好传说——高山流水、管鲍之交、三顾茅庐……习近平与贾大山的交往，堪称这些古代佳话的当代版本，洋溢着温暖动人的情感，让人深深地沉浸在一种至为美好的氛围中。

　　两人交往的整个过程，生动地印证和诠释了什么是朋友、什么是真正的友谊。伟大的友谊，总是建立在共同的理想追求的基础之上的。当时还很年轻的习近平同志的高洁远大的志向、平易近人的作风，对知识分子人才的爱惜尊重和心心相印，在作品中得到了生动的描绘。当时贾大山是县文化馆的一名创作人员，原本和习近平素昧平生，但习近平了解到贾大山是一位不图名利、德才兼备、不可多得的人才，便积极主动、坦诚友善地与之交往，并破格提拔任用。两人之间职位有差距，年龄、出身、生活经历等也有差距，但深刻的友谊弥合了这一切。从颇有些戏剧性的初次相识，逐渐发展到在交往中相知日深，彼此信任，再成为无话不谈、高度默契的战友兄弟般的深挚之情，两人的交往，自始至终都与私利毫无纠葛，而是基于共同的价值追求和人生信念，即都是用自己的才华和辛勤造福百姓，奉献社会。正是因为这点，两人才会互相欣赏，彼此引为人生道路上的知己。原本淡泊名利、无意仕途的贾大山，为年轻的习近平的崇高的理想信念和务实进取的工作作风所感动，"士为知己者死"，才以牺牲自己如日中天的文学事业为代价，出山担任了正定县文化局长，并在习近平为班长的县委领导班子的大力支持下，很短的时间内使当地的文化事业得到了飞速的发展。"二人同心，其利断金"，用《周易》中的这句话来比喻两人的真挚友谊所产生的效果，是十分恰切的。

真实生动地打捞和还原了一段湮没已久的故事，无疑体现了这篇作品的宝贵史料价值。但更为重要的，还应该是它所具有的现实映照和当下启发的意义。在年轻的习近平身上所体现出的那种全心全意、踏实勤勉的工作作风，那种与百姓情同手足的布衣情怀，正是充分地体现了党的领导干部应该具有的道德风范、品格修养。在党的群众路线教育实践活动正在深入推进的今天，从这篇作品中显然可以发掘出十分深刻的蕴涵。

作为一篇文学作品，这篇作品所呈现出的艺术质地也是颇为坚实绵密，值得称道。这个题材的独特性，使其最大限度地远离了想象和虚构。作家进行了深入扎实的采访，每一处场景，每一个情节，每一个细节，都有出处，有记载，有当事人的印证，可以说经得起历史的检验。但诸多的限制，并没有妨碍作者发挥自己的艺术才华。作者以普通人的视角，从细微之处着笔，写出了平淡后面的深意，写出了事物表象下面蕴含的情感、心绪、思想和韵味。两人之间的深厚情谊，就是通过一系列生动感人的细节描绘而得以体现的。像在无数个深夜，两人结束了促膝畅谈后，一个人要返回办公室或家里，而此时县委大院的门已经关了，于是一个人就俯下身子，给对方当梯子，翻越围墙；像习近平调走的前夜，两人结束了最后一次畅谈，贾大山抱着习近平办公室里的唐三彩骆驼和骏马回到家里，一言不发，倒头便睡，第二天中午仍然呆呆地发愣。这两个场景，就把两人之间深刻的默契，把贾大山心中的失落感，生动地展现了出来。这里没有煽情的描写，没有夸饰的词句，但读后分明能够强烈地感受到彼此间情感的深沉真挚。

　　《朋友——习近平与贾大山交往纪事》从谋篇布局到遣词造句，都经过了精心打磨，但读来却自然流畅。文字看似朴实无华，多以白描出之，却富有表现力。一些看似闲笔之处，其实也蓄积了张力，产生了书画中留白般的效果。如文章的结尾，作者在三十年后来到贾大山家里，在那间习近平和贾大山曾经无数次晤谈的屋子里，追忆往昔。房间里的布局和摆设一如当年，"恍恍惚惚中，我仿佛看到了当年的影子；隐隐约约里，我似乎听到了那时的笑声。唯有那两尊唐三彩骆驼和骏马，仍然新鲜如初，精神而挺拔地伫立着，伫立在时光的流影里，相互顾盼，心照不宣，像一对永恒的朋友……"这样的描写，虚实相生，今昔相连，在生活之"真"中捕捉到和描绘出了艺术之"美"，使读者获得了十分的审美愉悦。

　　概而言之，珍贵的史料性、生动的现实启示意义以及出色的文学表达，使得《朋友——习近平与贾大山交往纪事》成为一篇不可多得的纪实文学佳作，其价值必将随着时间的流逝而愈发凸显。

（作者系著名文艺评论家）

契合伟大时代的中国精神

——读纪实文学《朋友——习近平与贾大山交往纪事》有感

——

郑万里 张 雷

作家李春雷的纪实文学《朋友——习近平与贾大山交往纪事》（载于 2014 年 4 月 21 日《光明日报》头版头条）发表后，在海内外引起强烈反响。作品以现实主义笔调，深情地讲述了习近平与作家贾大山之间一段高山流水式的朋友情谊。这段故事浸透着古风佳话，揭示了一个朴素而发人深省的道理：领导干部交友不只是个人的事，更关乎党风、民风，以及国运兴衰；领导干部交友的价值取向，直接影响着整个社会。

突出了"厚德载物"的责任感和使命感

马克思对人的本质进行了科学概括："人的本质并不是单个人所固有的抽象物。在其现实性上，它是一切社会关系的总和。"人与人的交往构成社会关系。交往是人类特有的存在方式和活动方式，是人与人之间发生社会关系的一种介质。

这种介质的内涵，正如古人所云："天行健，君子以自强不息；地势坤，君子以厚德载物。"朋友之间的情感也应该用自强不息的精神来相互勉励、促进，以厚德载物的使命感来建立共同的人生目标和追求。朋友，是人的生命履历中最宝贵的情感财富，是人类社会相伴而行的群体细胞。

"习贾之交"自始至终彰显着"自强不息""厚德载物"的君子情怀，他们把友情建立在相互砥砺、共同追求的基础上，把共同的事业和共同的追求作为朋友交往的内在动力，充分显示出了志存高远的人生境界。

《朋友——习近平与贾大山交往纪事》中，作者写道："近平悄悄地坐下来，静心地听，耐心地等。"这充分表现了习近平的沉稳持重和优雅修养。

文中还披露，2009年7月号出版的期刊《散文百家》，整理发表了习近平2005年回正定考察时的录音："我记得刚见到贾大山同志，大山同志扭头一转就说：'来了个嘴上没毛的管我们！'"尽管这话是贾大山压低声说的，但依然可见他的快人快语。

这些段落读来情真意切、感人至深。尤其是这些故事发生在领导干部习近平和普通作家贾大山之间，其情感的震撼力就更加强烈。

这样的率性和随意，是两人友好交往的首要前提。他们在事业上，找到了共同的语言、兴趣、追求和友谊，堪称"君子之交"。这样的交往不因时空的变化而改变，反而历久弥新。习近平因工作调动去了福建，仍然挂念着远在河北正定的贾大山。当贾大山卧病不起时，习近平在百忙中抽出时间两次看望他，并守在病床前久久不忍离去。

习近平和贾大山的朋友之交，为我们交友树立了楷模。他们的友情没有当下人际关系中那种庸俗气，有的是精神上、心灵上的彼此相通；他们的友情没有当下人际关系中那种虚假气，有的是坦诚的沟通、信任和鼓励。他们用自己的真诚，书写了朋友的真实故事，演绎了崇德尚义的传世佳话。

"官德正则民风淳，官德毁则民风降。"全心全意为人民服务是党的根本宗旨。只有党风、政风、社会风气实现根本好转，达到常态化，全社会风清气正，才能为实现中华民族伟大复兴的中国梦提供必要的社会环境，奠定坚实的社会基础。

"习贾之交"的情感力量，与现实生活中那些异化了的人与人之间的关系，形成了明显对比。所以说，《朋友——习近平与贾大山交往纪事》是社会情感的净化剂，具有重大实践意义和社会价值。

彰显了以核心价值观为内涵的"中国精神"

中国士人历来有"先天下之忧而忧，后天下之乐而乐"的伟大情怀和"居庙堂之高则忧其民，处江湖之远则忧其君"的优良传统。30多年前，习近平、贾大山作为基层领导干部和普通的文化人，凭着坚定的理想信念、执着的学习精神、炽烈的工作热情和真挚的朋友情谊，激发出一种自强不息、进取求变的精神动力。

《朋友——习近平与贾大山交往纪事》写道："近平看书多且杂，更侧重于政治、哲学和经济，而大山尤专注于文学、史学和佛学；对于现实，近平是一个积极者，即使身处逆境，前途迷茫，他也始终乐观，胸怀梦想。当时，知识青年'返城热'余波未了，城市青年'出国热'高潮渐起，别人都在想方设法地回城或出国，他却主动申请回到农村去，从基层干起。而大山则是一个逍遥派，淡泊名利，无心仕途。他上学时未入团，上班后未入党。省作家协会多次调他去省城工作，他坚决不去，专门为他举办了一次作品研讨会，他居然没有出席。"

可见，志同道合的朋友是建立在心灵相通之上的，越是超越世俗的交往，情感越纯洁，友谊越深厚。习近平在《忆大山》一文中写道："大山有着洞察社会人生的深邃目光和独特视角……对人们反映强烈的一些社会问题，他往往有自己精辟独到、合情合理的意见和建议。"而在贾大山眼中，年轻的习近平知识渊博，而且对历史有着独到的见解。

这是一股舒展着的清新风气，必将影响到社会。朋友关系既属于社会关系范畴，必然受到社会风气的影响，也必然深刻影响着社会风气。社会风气实际上是一个宏观层面的有效评价指标。它表现在社会生活的各个领域，深刻影响着社会生活的发展和走向。社会风气始终需要高尚的精神去引领，使它成为社会发展的正能量。

"习贾之交"不仅仅是一位领导干部和一位知识分子的朋友交往，而且通过这个故事诠释了一个朴素而深刻的道理：一个人、一个民族、一个国家是要有点儿精神的。在当下中国，这种精神就是以爱国主义为核心的民族精神和以改革创新为核心的时代精神，合称中国精神。

习近平指出，中国精神是"凝心聚力的兴国之魂、强国之魂"。2013年5月

4日，他在同各界优秀青年代表座谈时指出："我们的国家，我们的民族，从积贫积弱一步一步走到今天的发展繁荣，靠的就是一代又一代人的顽强拼搏，靠的就是中华民族自强不息的奋斗精神。"

我们生活在一个伟大时代，伟大时代需要伟大精神。李春雷在谈到创作体会时说："在采访中，我深深地被一种精神所感动，他们那种勤于读书、善于学习，勤政廉政、干事创业、端正友谊、完善人格的精神，确实具有特殊的现实意义。后来我恍然大悟，这不就是中国精神吗？在创作中，我试图把这种精神内化在作品中，让它激励更多的人。"

在当下，弘扬这种精神应是责任和理想，一个有着强烈社会责任感的文学工作者，更要有无愧于伟大时代的远大理想和责任担当。

树立了领导干部交友的光辉典范

《朋友——习近平与贾大山交往纪事》发表之后，在社会上引起了强烈反响，媒体纷纷转载。这是因为作品抓住了"习贾之交"的精微，表现了真情、善感、美行，写出了精气神。

朋友，既有私交更有公务。在当今社会，"君子之交"似乎成了稀缺之物，有不少还是"酒肉之交""利益之交"，特别是个别领导干部把"交友"作为敛财或升迁的途径，严重地败坏了党风、政风和社会风气，破坏了社会主义市场经济体制的公平和正义原则。

"习贾之交"与这种风气形成了鲜明对比。他们在一起时主要谈工作、谈人生、谈志趣。习近平在回忆贾大山时说："在任期间，大山为正定文化事业的发展和古文物的研究、保护、维修、发掘、抢救，竭尽了自己的全力。常山影剧院、新华书店、电影院等文化设施的兴建和修复，隆兴寺大悲阁、天宁寺凌霄塔、开元寺钟楼、临济寺澄灵塔、广惠寺华塔、县文庙大成殿的修复，无不浸透着他辛劳奔走的汗水。"这既是对朋友的深情缅怀，也是对他们共同志趣的热情回忆，更是对当下端正党风、政风和社会风气的一种鞭策。

"习贾之交"表明，领导干部只有植根人民、造福人民，才能始终立于不败之地。习近平在党的十八大之后考察广东时强调："我们要尊重人民首创精神，在深入调查研究的基础上提出全面深化改革的顶层设计和总体规划，尊重实践、尊重创造、鼓励大胆探索、勇于开拓，聚合各项相关改革协调推进的正能量。"

这些观点，在《朋友——习近平与贾大山交往纪事》中亦有明显体现。文中有一段描写贾大山的段落尤其感人："春节期间，是别人最欢乐、最放松的时候，却正是他最紧张、最揪心的时刻。九处国保单位，全是砖木结构建筑，最易着火。每逢此时，他昼夜巡视，废寝忘食。别人劝他，他说：'祖宗的遗产，国家的宝物，我负责守护。出一点点问题，我就对不起正定，对不起县委，对不起习书记啊！'……"

习近平在《忆大山》一文中介绍了贾大山为人为官的作风："虽说他的淡泊名利是出了名的，可当起领导来却不含糊。上任伊始，他就下基层、访群众、查问题、定制度，几个月下来，便把原来比较混乱的文化系统整治得井井有条。"

领导干部应该有淡泊名利、宁静致远的情怀，应该有立党为公、执政为民的境界，应该有光明磊落、心系天下的胸襟，争取成为"三严三实"的人民公仆，真正肩负起实现中华民族伟大复兴的中国梦的历史使命。

展现了纪实文学独特的艺术魅力

"言之无文，行之不远。"普通的应景文字，可以图个一时之快，但难以长久，更无法传世。而真正的文学精品，是写给当代的，写给世界的，更是写给历史。纪实文学作为传统的史传文学样式，自古以来就是中国文学的脊梁。从《战国策》《左传》到《史记》，现代文学史上的《包身工》《1936年春在太原》《白门秋柳》《冀中一日》和《西行漫记》，到当代的《县委书记的榜样——焦裕禄》《哥德巴赫猜想》《扬眉剑出鞘》《根本利益》《寻找巴金的黛莉》和《木棉花开》等，无不展示出纪实文学的独特魅力——真实感人的艺术震撼力和强大的社会影响力。

《朋友——习近平与贾大山交往纪事》的创作也是如此。在严格坚守真实性的同时，作者特别注意调动各种艺术表现手法。在整体行文叙事中，作家借鉴了古典小说、古典散文的笔法，变换视角，延伸思绪，杂以闲笔，多用短句；在结构布局上，作家追求自然、浑圆的感觉，看似随意，实则有心。

比如细节处理。那一对唐三彩骆驼和马，三处出现，都有特殊用意。第一处，是在习近平办公室，"成群的书们，或躺在桌面上，或站在窗台上。屋内最醒目的物品，是窗台上的两尊仿制唐三彩：一峰骆驼和一匹骏马，那是北京朋友赠送的纪念品。"在这里，说明习近平有着很多真情朋友。这是朋友赠送的，将来又赠送给朋友贾大山，真情传递，温暖人心。第二处是送别时，大山抱着习近平的两件特殊赠品回家。在这里，作家并没有写赠送的过程，因为那样写免不了要虚构对话等，会降低其真实性。这样处理，删繁就简，更含蓄、更真实、更感人。第三处，是文章结尾，作家坐在两人当年经常会面的小屋里，大山走了，但唐三彩依然挺立在时光流影里，崭新如故，虽然默默无言，却寄寓着友谊永恒，真情永远。

在语言运用上，《朋友——习近平与贾大山交往纪事》简洁而精妙，蕴藉而饱满，自然成态，芳香浓郁，充分展现了现代白话文的神韵和魅力。

在作品的思想性上，作家也有着更多的"用心"。作为一个具有强烈责任心的现实主义作家，李春雷试图给社会大众，特别是官场提供一些思考。比如，不管是从勤于读书、善于学习，尊重知识、尊重人才的角度看，还是从严于修身、完善人格，勤政廉政、干事创业的角度看，"习贾之交"都具有重要的现实意义。而如果从当前正在开展的党的群众路线教育实践活动的角度看，就更有借鉴意义了。

所以说，《朋友——习近平与贾大山交往纪事》作为一篇思想性、艺术性结合完美的纪实文学作品，充分展现了纪实文学独特的艺术魅力。

"习贾之交"是一段值得称颂的真情故事，是古代经典故事在现实生活中的延续和提升，它会像高山流水、管鲍之交、三顾茅庐等历史上的著名成语故事一样，为中华文明史留下一段佳话。网络上已经有人注册名词"习贾之交"，相信会有一个更恰当、更准确的成语，把这个故事表达出来，流传下去。

（原载《光明日报》2014 年 6 月 9 日）

精妙的文学名篇

——读李春雷纪实文学《朋友》有感

——

关仁山

李春雷的纪实文学《朋友——习近平与贾大山交往纪事》一经发表，便在全社会产生巨大反响。《人民日报》《光明日报》《河北日报》《新华文摘》等数百家报刊予以转载和评论，中宣部《活页文选》重点推出，中国言实出版社又出版了两种单行本，上海海派连环画中心也正在积极准备改编成连环画……这种情形，用盛况空前来形容，也不算过分。

《朋友》之所以誉满天下，除了题材重大之外，其展现的精妙绝伦的艺术风格，也是重要原因。

近年来，不少报告文学作品让人诟病，究其原因，还是"广告"多，"歌德"多，浮光掠影，粗制滥造。但是，作为鲁迅文学奖历史上最年轻的报告文学作家，李春雷在报告文学，特别是短篇报告文学创作上独辟蹊径，大胆探索，走出了一条极富特色的创新之路。

著名诗人、评论家叶延滨曾就此专门撰文《报告文学的文体思考》，特别指出李春雷作品的文本意义，即报告文学应首先具备"报告"的特性（真实性）；在此基础上，又必须是向读者进行"文学报告"（艺术性）；再就是报告文学应该惜墨如金，不宜片面追求大篇幅。对此我十分有同感。 从春雷近时期的短篇创作来看，他确实是在努力追求、实践和实现着这样一个目标，这在《朋友》的创作中体现得更加充分。

由于春雷长期自觉沉浸于中国古典散文、古典小说的熏陶浸润，有很好的散文功底，所以作品语言清新洒脱而又极富韵律，结构浑然天成而又开合自如。精致、富于表现力的白描又使他寥寥几笔就可以勾勒出人物性格、环境特点，使人感觉到明清白话小说刻画描写之韵味。有人说贾樟柯是把电影（故事）当作纪录片来拍，那么我要说，读李春雷的报告文学可以得到古典散文小说的享受。这种鲜明的艺术特征在《朋友》中俯拾即是，熠熠生辉。

如写贾大山耿直、孤傲、狷介，是"高高大大""清清瘦瘦"，"博闻强记，口才极佳"。写第一次见面的波折，大胆而又不失分寸，正是大家手笔。

写习近平，"穿着一件褪色的绿军装，虽然态度谦恭，满脸微笑，但毕竟年轻啊，像一名普通的退伍兵，又像一个青涩的文学青年。""悄悄地坐下来，精心地听，耐心地等。"着墨不多却十分传神。写近平的办公室，简洁而富有深意："只有一间屋子，两条板凳支起一个床铺，一张三屉桌，两把砖红色椅子，一个暖瓶，一盏灯泡。没有书架，成群的书们，或躺在桌面上，或站在窗台上。屋内最醒目的物品，是窗台上的两尊仿制唐三彩：一峰骆驼和一匹骏马，那是北京朋友赠送的纪念品。"年轻好学又沉稳朴实，虚怀若谷而意志坚定——鲜明、立体、可亲的美好形象跃然纸上。

贾大山的家宴，则又是另一番景象：简朴而不失热情好客，罗列琳琅而清爽雅致："大山准备了几个精致的小菜：雪里蕻炒肉、莲藕片、花生米和凉调菜心。主食呢，就是涮羊肉。没有专用火锅，把铝盆放在蜂窝炉上，权当涮器。虽然器具简陋，但材料绝不含糊：麻酱、韭花、蒜末、香菜、酱豆腐一应俱全。"

写大山和近平的离别，采取侧面映衬，避实就虚："那天晚上，大山回来时，怀里抱着两尊唐三彩：一峰骆驼和一匹骏马。他一言不发，倒头便睡，直到第二天中午。起床后仍是呆呆地发愣。妻子以为他病了，催他吃药。他摇摇头，慢慢地说一句：'习书记调走了。'"——这样写，人物，动作，语言，心理，言简意赅，恰到好处。唐三彩两次出现，前后照应，点染了情节，完善了结构，凸显了友情。更重要的，是巧妙留白，删繁就简，实写大山回家，虚写道别的场景，既有效恪守了报告文学绝对真实的原则，又给读者留下足够的想象空间，堪称老道蕴藉。

　　纵观《朋友》，作者调动各种艺术表现手法：在整体行文叙述上，借鉴吸收古典小说、古典散文的笔法，变换视角，延伸思绪，杂以闲笔，多用短句；在结构布局上，空间切换，远近结合，追求自然、圆浑的效果，看似随意，实则有心，创造出瑰丽的艺术效果，充分展示了李春雷报告文学的魅力。读这样的作品，没有迟滞感、生涩感，有的是娓娓道来的叙述、生动感人的情节，情感细致入微，人物质感丰满。作品所产生的巨大艺术感染力，沁人心脾，震撼人心。

　　细览篇幅，仅八千余字。可以说是以小见大，以少总多，简短精约，如连城玉璧，温润晶莹又光彩夺目。这较之于应景附和制作，判若云泥，立分高下。刘勰说"以少总多，情貌无遗"。刘知几说"睹一事于句中，反三隅于句外"。王安石则有诗句"浓绿万枝红一点，动人春色不须多"。讲的都是这个道理。

　　我们呼唤既是"报告"，又是"文学"的报告文学精品。因此可以说，李春雷在这方面的实践具有很强、很有针对性的现实价值。从这个意义上讲，我们完全可以做出这样的判断：以《朋友》为代表的李春雷系列精短报告文学创作，具有里程碑式的重要意义。

　　　　　　　　　　　　　　　　　　　（作者系河北省作家协会主席、著名作家）